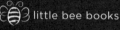 little bee books

New York, NY
Copyright © 2023 by Little Bee Books
All rights reserved, including the right of
reproduction in whole or in part in any form.
Library of Congress Cataloging-in-Publication
Data is available upon request.

Manufactured in China TPL 1222

ISBN 978-1-4998-1366-1 (hardcover)
First Edition 10 9 8 7 6 5 4 3 2 1
ISBN 978-1-4998-1365-4 (paperback)
First Edition 10 9 8 7 6 5 4 3 2 1
ISBN 978-1-4998-1367-8 (ebook)

littlebeebooks.com

For information about special discounts on bulk purchases, please contact Little Bee Books at sales@littlebeebooks.com.

THE ALIEN NEXT DOOR

THE SURPRISE SLEEPOVER

by A. I. Newton
illustrated by Alan Brown

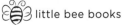
little bee books

TABLE OF CONTENTS

HOME!

A SPACESHIP APPROACHED Earth, getting ready to land. On board were Zeke and his parents, Xad and Quar, aliens from the planet Tragas. They were returning to their temporary home—Earth. Also on board were Zeke's human best friends, Harris and Roxy, who were on their way back home after an unexpected trip to Tragas.

Xad and Quar were planetary researchers. They had recently completed their research of Earth. Their work was being displayed at the Museum of Galactic Culture on the planet Kretlak Prime. They had just stopped there to view the exhibit on their way back.

Everyone was on the ship's bridge looking out the front viewscreen. All they could see was a thick bank of clouds as they dropped through Earth's atmosphere.

"Prepare the holo-cloaking display," Quar said, just before they broke through the cloud cover.

"Engaging now," said Xad.

"What's the holo-cloaking display?" Harris asked.

"It hides the ship from anyone on the planet below by projecting another image," Zeke explained. "We use it whenever we land on a new planet so no one knows we have arrived."

"So that's why no one knew that aliens had landed on Earth back when you first came here," said Roxy.

"No one but me!" said Harris.

The three friends laughed. Harris recalled that when Zeke first arrived on Earth, he tried his best to prove that Zeke was an alien. In time Zeke revealed that Harris's suspicions were correct, and the two became great friends.

"The holo-cloaking display is projecting the image of a thunderstorm to anyone looking up from Earth's surface. All they'll see are thick, dark clouds and flashes of lightning," explained Quar.

Hidden by the projection of a thunderstorm, the ship broke through the cloud layer revealing the ground below to those on board.

"There's my house!" Roxy said excitedly, pointing at the viewscreen.

"And there's mine!" shouted Harris.

"Prepare for final landing," said Quar, adjusting the ship's navigation controls.

The ship gently touched down in Zeke's backyard, next to a long wooden fence. It landed in the spot where a rusty old garden shed had stood.

"Zeke—you, your mother, and I must take on our human forms again before we leave the ship," said Xad.

"Right!" said Zeke. "It's been so long since we've had to change out of our true Tragonian forms I almost forgot."

Zeke, Xad, and Quar all begin to morph from their natural, green-skinned, tentacled Tragonian forms.

When Xad finished changing, he had a human-looking arm growing out of his head. When Quar was done, she had two eyes bulging out of her back. Zeke ended up with human-style ears on the front of his face where his eyes should have been.

"I guess it *has* been a while since we had to take on human shape," said Xad. "We all have to concentrate a little harder."

Focusing, the three Tragonians completed the transformation into their human forms.

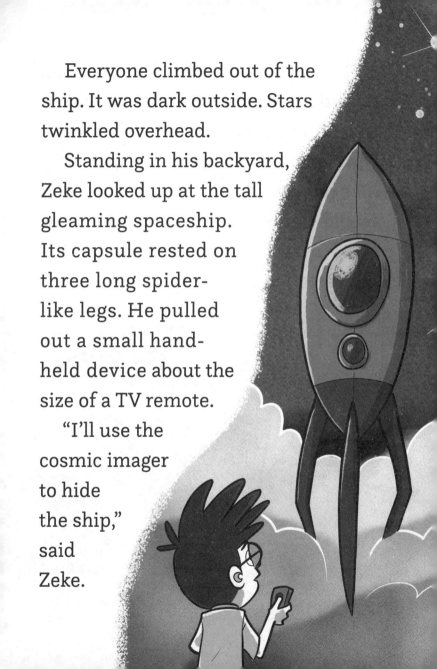

Everyone climbed out of the ship. It was dark outside. Stars twinkled overhead.

Standing in his backyard, Zeke looked up at the tall gleaming spaceship. Its capsule rested on three long spider-like legs. He pulled out a small hand-held device about the size of a TV remote.

"I'll use the cosmic imager to hide the ship," said Zeke.

He pressed a button and the ship started to rumble. It glowed bright green and began to reassemble itself. The capsule and legs of the spaceship changed into the rusty metal walls of an old garden shed. When the glow faded away, the ship was gone and the shed stood in its place.

"According to the ship's chrono-log, exactly one hour has passed here on Earth since we left," Xad explained.

"I thought it would only be thirty minutes," Roxy said.

"It seems that our detour to the Museum of Galactic Culture added the extra half hour," said Quar.

"Well, for me it's been weeks!" said Roxy. "I miss my parents—and some good old Earth food! Thanks for the awesome trip. I'll see you guys later." Roxy ran off toward home.

"Me too," said Harris. "I don't want my folks to worry, even if it's only been an hour to them." Harris also headed to his house, which was right next door.

Zeke watched as his friends left, realizing that this time, he would really have to say goodbye to them—forever!

2 BACK ON EARTH

HARRIS BURST THROUGH the front door of his house.

"Mom! Dad! I'm home," he shouted.

"Harris?" said his Mom, meeting him in the front hallway. "I was wondering where you've been."

"Oh, I was just hanging out with Roxy and Zeke," he explained, telling the truth but leaving out the part about visiting other planets.

"Did you get caught in that terrible thunderstorm?" his Mom asked.

"Well, I—" Harris started, but wasn't quite sure what to say. *She must have seen the image of the thunderstorm projected from the ship.*

"You're completely dry!" said his Mom, mussing his hair.

"I, um, well actually, I was just next door at Zeke's," Harris said, thinking fast. "We were playing a video game about traveling in a rocket ship to a distant planet. I guess we were so caught up in the game, I didn't even notice the storm. By the time I left, it was over."

"Well, I have some dinner ready for you," said his Mom. "Come on."

Harris followed his Mom into the kitchen and spotted a steaming bowl of spaghetti. *Human food!* he thought. *Yum!*

Meanwhile, Zeke and his parents were back in their house.

"It actually feels nice to be back on Earth," said Zeke.

"Well, don't get too comfortable, Zekelabraxis," said Xad, using Zeke's full Tragonian name. "Your mother and I must return to Tragas as soon as we can to receive our next research assignment."

"I know," Zeke said, feeling sad and a little nervous.

The reality of leaving his good friends was really sinking in.

New planet, new school, new kids, new friends . . . I hope. Here I go again, he thought.

"When are we leaving?" he asked.

"We need to draw power from the Earth's sun all day tomorrow to recharge the ship's Barzium crystals. Then we can take off for the trip home to Tragas the following morning," Xad explained.

The day after tomorrow! thought Zeke. *That only gives me one day to spend hanging out with Roxy and Harris!*

"In fact," Xad continued, "please assist me in setting up the Barzium charging system so it will be ready when the sun rises tomorrow."

Zeke and Xad headed outside. They opened the creaky, squeaky, rusted metal door of the "shed" and stepped inside.

Xad slid open a panel in the shed's wall, revealing what looked like two glowing purple buttons.

"Barzium crystals, the heart of our spaceship," Xad said proudly. "The only place in the galaxy they can be found is deep in the Barzantak Mountains on Tragas."

Xad moved to the other side of the shed and picked up a stack of rectangular panels.

"These will collect energy from the Earth's sun all day tomorrow," Xad explained. "When that energy is run through a Radion Converter, it changes the sunlight into power that the Barzium crystals can store.

"Zekelabraxis, please open that storage container and hand me the Radion Converter," Xad said.

Zeke opened a large steel box. He pulled out a chrome and glass device about the size of a microwave.

"Excellent," said Xad. "Now help me attach these energy collector panels to the roof of the shed."

Zeke and Xad carried the panels outside. Zeke climbed up on the roof of the shed and Xad handed him the panels, one by one. Zeke used suction connectors to secure the panels to the shed's roof.

"To Earth people, these will look like the regular solar panels they use to create electricity," Xad explained.

They ran a wire from the panels back into the shed. That wire was then connected to the Radion Converter, which was then connected to the Barzium crystals.

"There," said Xad. "The Barzium crystals should be fully charged by tomorrow evening. Then, the next morning, we will take off for home."

Home, thought Zeke. *It's funny. I feel like I just* got *home!*

THE FOLLOWING MORNING, Zeke got up early. He ran outside and saw the backyard shed once again transformed into the Tragonian spaceship. His parents were inside, busy making preparations to leave for Tragas the next day.

We're really going back to Tragas! he thought. *This will be my last day on Earth.*

Zeke joined his parents inside the ship. They moved from control station to control station, entering information into the ship's navigation systems.

Panels flashed long series of numbers. Lights blinked on and off. Large screens showed star fields swirling in space.

A small, flying robot zoomed right past Zeke's head and zipped over to an open control panel. Tiny arms holding tools popped from the robot's round body and began making adjustments.

"I see that the Bot-Drones are on the job," Zeke said, stepping out of the way of two more, who flew right past him. Quar noticed that Zeke looked very sad.

"Zekelabraxis, why don't you go and spend some time with Harris and Roxy before we leave tomorrow," she said. "You don't want to go without saying goodbye to your friends."

"Agreed," said Xad. "We know that they made your time on Earth much easier."

Zeke nodded and turned toward the ship's hatch to leave.

Suddenly, a display screen blazed to life, projected in the air above his parents' heads.

The word *URGENT!* flashed across the screen. Zeke and his parents looked up.

"Well, who could be contacting us here?" Quar wondered.

"Let us find out," said Xad. "Open transmission!"

A message addressed to Zeke's parents floated in midair:

Xad and Quar,

It is critically important that you meet me on Mars before the end of this Earth day. I am traveling from Tragas and should arrive on Mars by 17:35:15 Standard Galactic Time. Please acknowledge that you have received this and can meet with me.

Sincerely, Naxtik Frow, Supervisor, Tragonian Research Institute

"What can be so urgent that Supervisor Frow is coming all the way from Tragas to speak with us?" Xad asked.

Zeke could tell that his father sounded worried.

"I can't imagine," said Quar. "Our mission to Earth was a great success. Supervisor Frow knows that the Museum of Galactic Culture featured our research."

"Hmm . . ." said Xad. "Why would she come all the way to this solar system? Usually, she would meet with us back on Tragas to give us our next assignment. This clearly changes our plans. We are almost ready for our scheduled takeoff tomorrow. But it looks like we will need to leave today once the ship is charged, spend the night on Mars, and then return to Earth to pick you up tomorrow."

"So, I'm not going with you?" asked Zeke.

"Unnecessary," replied Xad.

"I don't like the idea of Zekelabraxis staying in the house alone," said Quar.

"Maybe I can stay with Harris," said Zeke.

"Excellent suggestion," said Xad.

"Great!" said Zeke, happy to get more time with his friend. "I'll go talk to him now!"

4 A CHANGE IN PLANS

ZEKE RUSHED OVER TO Harris's house.

"So I guess this is goodbye . . . for real," Harris said sadly, when the two boys were alone in Harris's room.

"Actually," Zeke said, smiling. "Not quite yet."

Zeke filled Harris in on the message his parents got from their boss.

"Mars!" exclaimed Harris. "Wow. How long will it take them to get there?"

"I think only a few hours," said Zeke. "But they are leaving today and they won't get back to Earth until tomorrow. My parents don't want me staying by myself overnight. Do you think I could stay at your house?"

A big smile spread across Harris's face. "Sleepover!" he shouted.

Zeke looked puzzled.

"Sleep over what?" he asked.

"You mean they don't have sleepovers on Tragas?" Harris asked.

"Well, sometimes I sleep hanging upside down from the ceiling," Zeke said, "so I guess I'd be sleeping *over* the floor, but I don't see what—"

"On Earth, when a friend sleeps over at another friend's house, it's called a 'sleepover,'" Harris explained.

"Oh, you mean a copodnix," said Zeke, using the Tragonian word for sleepover. "I have had many a copodnix with my friends back on Tragas. It's a lot of fun."

"Come on," said Harris. "Let's go ask my parents if we can have a copodnix . . . I mean a sleepover here tonight!"

Harris and Zeke raced downstairs. They found Harris's parents in the living room. They explained that Zeke's parents had to go on an overnight trip and asked if it would be okay if Zeke spent the night.

"Of course," said Harris's mom.

"A good old-fashioned sleepover, huh?" said Harris's dad.

"Maybe we can invite Roxy, too?" Harris asked.

"Sure," said his mom. "I'm so happy that you three have become such good friends."

"Thanks, Mom!" said Harris.

"Yes, thank you, Mrs. Walker," said Zeke. "I'll go tell my parents that I'll be sleeping over here."

"Great!" said Harris. "I'll call Roxy."

Zeke hurried over to his backyard and climbed aboard the spaceship.

"It's all set," he told his parents, who were getting ready for takeoff. "I can stay at Harris's house tonight for a sleepover."

"What will you be sleeping over?" asked Xad.

"No, 'sleepover' is just the Earth name for a copodnix," Zeke explained. "Harris is going to see if Roxy can join us, too."

"Oh," said Quar. "That should be fun. What a perfect way to spend your last night on Earth, and the last time you will hang on with Harris and Roxy."

"It's 'hang *out*', but yes, it should be fun," said Zeke.

"It is time for us to take off for Mars, Zekelabraxis," said Xad.

"Okay," said Zeke, heading for the spaceship's exit. "Have a good trip. I hope everything goes well with Supervisor Frow."

"Yes," said Xad. "I hope so."

Zeke could hear the worry in his father's voice. He climbed out of the ship and stood aside as the engines flared to life.

As the ship lifted into the sky, a sudden thunderstorm moved in, hiding the takeoff.

5 LAST DAY TOGETHER

WHEN ZEKE ARRIVED, HE found Roxy waiting with Harris.

"I'm so glad you could be here for my last day on Earth, Roxy," said Zeke.

"You make it sound so gloomy," Roxy said, laughing. "But, of course, I wouldn't miss it! I just hope everything is all right with your folks. They were so nice to me on the ship, and on Tragas, and at the museum."

"Yes, they are concerned about why their boss is coming all the way from Tragas to talk with them," Zeke said. "Normally, we'd just go back to Tragas and their supervisor would give them their next assignment. And then it'd be off to a new planet for all of us."

"Do you think they might be in trouble?" Harris asked.

"Do you think someone found out that Harris and I were on Tragas and at the museum?" Roxy asked, sounding worried. "I know we really weren't supposed to be there."

"Oh, gee," said Harris. "I sure hope that we didn't get them in trouble."

"I don't know," said Zeke.

Everyone got quiet. Harris decided to lighten the mood.

"Oh, good news. Roxy can join our copodnix tonight!" he said.

"Our *what*?" asked Roxy.

"It's the Tragonian word for 'sleepover,'" Harris explained.

"Oh," said Roxy. "Well, whatever you call it, it's going to be great!"

"But first, we have all day to be together," said Zeke, also trying to brighten the mood. "What should we do?"

"I have an idea," said Harris. "Roxy has never seen you really use your powers. We were always so busy keeping your secret. But now that she knows all about you, let's have some fun!"

Harris ran into his garage and came out holding a frisbee and a basketball.

"Come on, let's go to the park!"

The three friends went to a nearby park. They spread out in an open grassy area and formed a triangle.

"Now, you remember how to toss this, right?" Harris asked, holding up the frisbee.

"I think so," said Zeke.

"Let me show you again," said Harris.

He gripped the frisbee and snapped his wrist. It sailed through the air in a straight line right toward Roxy. She snatched the spinning disc out of the air, then sent it spinning back to Harris, who caught it.

"Ready?" Harris asked Zeke.

He nodded.

Harris tossed the frisbee at Zeke, who reached up and snatched it out of the air.

"Nice catch!" said Roxy. "Now try a throw."

Gripping the frisbee the way Harris had taught him, Zeke attempted a throw. The disc spun off wildly and bounced along the ground.

"I got it!" Zeke shouted, trotting toward the fallen frisbee.

He picked it up and tried another toss. This one bounced off a nearby tree and crashed to the ground.

Harris picked up the disc and looked around.

"I don't think anyone is watching," he said. "Why don't you show Roxy what you can do, Zeke?"

Harris tossed the frisbee to Zeke, who again made a nice catch.

Zeke tossed the frisbee toward Roxy. It started to spin off wildly, heading toward a nearby pond.

Zeke closed his eyes and placed his fingertips on his head. Suddenly, the frisbee curved away from the pond, rising into the air. It zipped through the branches of a tree, did a loop-the-loop in midair, and glided right into Roxy's hand.

"Wow!" she said. "That was amazing!"

"Told you!" said Harris. "Now you know why it was so hard to keep the truth about Zeke a secret for so long."

After a few more frisbee tosses and tricks, the friends decided to head over to the basketball courts.

"Wait until you see what Zeke can do with a basketball!" said Harris.

6
HOOPS AND MONSTERS

THE THREE FRIENDS HEADED over to the park's basketball courts.

Roxy shot first. The ball swished right through the hoop.

Harris went next and banked it in off the backboard.

Then it was Zeke's turn.

"Remember what we talked about the last time we played, Zeke," said Harris. "Set your feet, look at the back of the hoop, then launch the ball, pushing with your wrist."

Zeke took the ball and launched a shot—which sailed over the backboard and crashed into a fence.

"A little too much wrist, I think," said Harris.

Zeke chased after the ball, then tossed it to Roxy, who hit her next shot.

"Okay, Zeke, normally I wouldn't say this, but try again—this time using your powers," Harris said.

Zeke looked around to make sure that no one was watching, then launched another shot, this time using less force. The ball was about to fall short, when it suddenly lifted up and dropped down perfectly through the hoop.

"I really see how you could win in every sport," said Roxy, thinking back to when they played baseball for the Chargers. "But why don't we play something that you *can't* use your powers to win?"

"Like what?" Zeke asked.

"Well, how about some video games at the arcade?" Roxy said.

"Yeah," said Harris. "I heard they just got the latest version of *Monster Mayhem*. I've been dying to try it."

"I'm happy to do anything, as long as the three us of are together," said Zeke, trying hard not to think about leaving his friends tomorrow.

A short time later, they arrived at the arcade. Beeps, boops, and explosions sounded all around. Bells ringing, electronic music playing, and excited kids shouting and laughing filled the large room.

The line at the brand new *Monster Mayhem* machine was the longest in the whole arcade. The three friends waited patiently for their turn.

"So how do you play *Monster Mayhem*?" Zeke asked.

"A group of terrible monsters invades a town," Harris explained. "Each player has a laser cage launcher."

"That's right," Roxy continued. "The object of the game is to launch a laser cage at each monster and trap it inside. When you have trapped all the monsters, they disappear, the town is safe, and you win the game!"

"Reminds me of the baby Kraka Beast hunt back on Tragas," Zeke said.

"Wow," said Roxy. "They made a video game out of hunting baby Kraka Beasts?"

"No, it is not a game," said Zeke. "It's real life. On Tragas, hunters use a sonic zar-net to capture baby Kraka Beasts that have gotten too close to a city in order to return them to their natural home in the wild."

A few minutes later, their turn came. Roxy went first. She chased a multiheaded monster through the streets. She fired her laser cage launcher at the beast, but it outran her each time.

"Wow, I was pretty good at the last version of the game, but this one is way harder!" she said.

Harris was up next. He followed a long-fanged creature down a dark alley. Just as he launched his laser cage, the beast climbed straight up a brick wall and got away.

Then it was Zeke's turn. He chased a powerful hairy beast through the streets until he had it trapped inside an empty warehouse.

"Too bad you can't use your powers to guide the cage onto the monster," said Harris.

"Maybe not," Zeke said, "but I *can* use my power to increase my hand-eye coordination."

Zeke placed his hands on either side of his head. He narrowed his eyes, focusing all his energy on the video game screen in front of him. The monster appeared, running through the warehouse.

Waiting until the exact right moment, Zeke pressed the launch button on the controller. His laser cage dropped down, trapping the monster. A red light on top of the video game machine started flashing and a bell rang, signaling a winner.

Everyone in the arcade paused for a moment and applauded Zeke's win.

"Wow," said Roxy. "I guess you can use your power for almost anything you set your mind to!"

"Nice going, Zeke," said Harris. "But I think we should head home. My folks said that we could have an early pizza dinner, so we could start our sleepover sooner!"

"Great!" said Roxy.

"Yes," added Zeke. "It is sleepover time. And I have really missed that Earth delicacy you call pizza!"

7 SLEEPOVER TIME

WHEN THE THREE FRIENDS arrived at Harris's house, his folks had several pizzas waiting.

"We're so glad you three could have this sleepover before Zeke has to go home to . . . um, what was the name of the place you're from again, Zeke?" asked Harris's mom.

"Uh, I'm from Tragas," Zeke said, somewhat nervously. He glanced at Roxy and Harris and saw that they looked uncomfortable, too.

"I never could find that on any map," said Harris's dad.

"It's pretty far from here," Harris said quickly. Then, just as quickly, he changed the subject. "This is great pizza. Thanks, Mom!"

After dinner, the three friends headed up to Harris's room. Three sleeping bags sat rolled up on the floor.

"What do we do now?" Zeke asked.

"Well, what kinds of things do you do at a copodnix on Tragas?" Roxy asked.

"Let's see," Zeke said, thinking. "We play Rutnaq, where we mind-project small objects into the air above us, then move them around a virtual path, jumping in front of each other, all trying to get to the end of the path first."

"Sounds like Race and Chase," said Roxy. "That's my favorite board game!"

"Just what I was thinking!" added Harris.

He reached under his bed and pulled out a stack of board games. Right on top was the game called Race and Chase. Harris flipped the lid off, pulled out the game board, and spilled the game pieces onto the floor.

"Since you are the only one who can mind-project, we'll have to play the Earth version of Rutnaq—a board game," Harris said.

"We still move around a path, jumping in front of each other, but we use our hands to move metal pieces around this game board," Roxy explained.

Everyone sat cross-legged on the floor. Roxy reached out and grabbed a small metal piece shaped like a sailboat. "I'm the sailboat!" Roxy announced.

"You're always the sailboat every time we play!" Harris whined.

Roxy shrugged. "I like sailboats," she said.

"I'll be the race car," Harris said, picking up the race car shaped piece.

Zeke looked over the remaining pieces scattered on the floor.

"I guess I'll be the rocket ship," he said, picking up that piece.

"Seems right," Roxy said, smiling.

Harris grabbed a pair of dice and rolled. He got a five and a three.

"So, you add up the numbers shown on the two dice, then move that amount of spaces around the board," Harris explained. He moved his race car eight spaces.

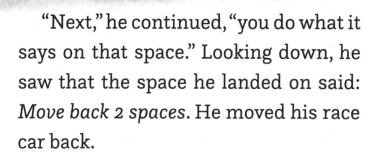

"Next," he continued, "you do what it says on that space." Looking down, he saw that the space he landed on said: *Move back 2 spaces*. He moved his race car back.

Roxy went next. She rolled a four. Moving her sailboat four spaces, she landed on a space that said: *Move ahead 2 spaces*.

"Aha!" she said. "That puts me on the same space as Harris. And in this game, whenever you land on a space where another player's piece is, you jump past them and move your piece to the space right in front of them."

"Your turn, Zeke," said Harris. "Although tossing dice may not be as much fun as mind projecting."

"Well," said Zeke, "it could be."

He rolled the dice and got a ten. Lifting his hands up to his head and closing his eyes, Zeke made his small metal rocket ship lift off from the starting spot. It flew over the board and landed on space ten.

"Funny," said Roxy.

Zeke smiled.

"Your space says, 'Move ahead two spaces,'" Harris read. "You're in the lead."

"I think I like this game," said Zeke as Harris picked up the dice for his next turn.

8 MOVIES AND JUNK FOOD

THE GAME CONTINUED UNTIL Zeke got to the finish line first.

He was so pleased that he used his power to lift all three game pieces into the air. The three friends laughed as the rocket ship chased the race car and the sailboat around Harris's room.

"How about a movie?" asked Harris.

"Sure," said Zeke. "What do you want to watch?"

"What about *The World Beneath the Sea*?" asked Roxy. "It's all about the really amazing creatures that live in the ocean."

"You mean like *Danger in the Deep*, that really scary 4-D holo-projection movie we watched at my house?" asked Zeke. "There were some cool undersea monsters in that one."

"This is even better," said Roxy, "because all the creatures in this movie are real!"

"Wow!" said Zeke. "I guess I don't know anything about the animals that live in Earth's oceans."

"Well, you're going to love this!" said Harris, setting up the movie.

"Hey, what kind of sleepover is this?" asked Roxy. "Where's the junk food?"

"Right!" said Harris. "I'll be right back."

Harris bolted downstairs. He returned a few minutes later with bags of chips, cookies, doughnuts, spongy, cream-filled bars, cheese puffs, and other junk food.

"Now we can watch a movie!" said Roxy.

Harris started the movie and Zeke was amazed by the colorful, strange creatures living in Earth's oceans.

"What is that?" he asked pointing at a multitentacled creature moving through the sea.

"It's called an octopus," said Roxy. "It has eight tentacles."

"Wow, that's even more than me," Zeke said. He grabbed a bag of cheese puffs and shoved a few into his mouth. Then he looked at his fingers and saw that they were completely covered with orange powder. "What happened to my fingers?" he asked.

"That's the best part of eating cheese puffs!" said Harris. "After you eat them you get to lick your fingers and kind of eat them again!"

Zeke licked the orange powder off his fingers and turned back to the movie.

He "oohed" and "ahhed" at the rainbow of undersea life swimming through the ocean.

Suddenly the screen was filled by the biggest creature Zeke had ever seen.

"What's that?!" he asked.

"A blue whale," said Roxy. "The biggest animal on Earth!"

Zeke's eyes opened wide as he followed the mighty blue whale. It rose from the ocean  and burst out into the sunshine!

"I feel like my parents missed a whole bunch of Earth life in their research by not studying all the creatures that live in the sea," Zeke said. "I wish they had more time here."

The mood in the room darkened. The three friends had been having so much fun, the reality of Zeke leaving the next day had left their minds. They grew quiet now as they watched the rest of the movie.

When the movie ended, Roxy spoke up.

"All right," she said. "Enough gloom and doom. I know exactly what we need to cheer us up—a game of Truth or Dare!"

9 TRUTH OR DARE

"WHAT'S TRUTH OR DARE?" asked Zeke.

"It's a game where we ask each other to either tell the truth or dare each other to do something," explained Roxy.

"What a strange thing to do," said Zeke. "And you say this is a game?"

"Yup, I'll show you," Roxy said. Then she turned to Harris. "Okay, Harris, Truth or Dare!"

"Truth," said Harris.

"Okay," said Roxy. "Harris, when was the last time you cleaned up your room?"

Harris looked around his room. Stuff was scattered everywhere—clothes, toys, books.

"Well, sometime last month, I guess," Harris said sheepishly.

"That, I definitely believe is the truth," said Roxy.

"Okay, my turn," Harris said turning to Zeke. "Zeke, Truth or Dare?"

"Dare?" said Zeke, sounding uncertain, still puzzled by this Earth game.

"Okay, Zeke, I dare you to lick your elbow," Harris said.

Zeke moved his arm up toward his mouth. He stuck out his tongue but couldn't reach his elbow.

Then he got an idea.

He changed his human arm into one of his very bendable Tragonian tentacles. Then he easily lifted the tentacle up to his mouth and licked it.

"I can see that Zeke might have an advantage in this game, too," Harris said. "Okay, Zeke, your turn to ask Roxy."

"Okay, Roxy, Truth or Dare?" Zeke asked.

"Truth," said Roxy.

"Roxy, if you could have powers beyond what humans can do, what power would you want to have?" Zeke asked.

"Oh, that's easy," said Roxy. "I'd love to be able to fly."

"Really?" asked Zeke. "Well, I can help you with that."

Zeke closed his eyes and put his fingertips against his head. Suddenly, Roxy lifted off the floor and flew up to the ceiling.

"This is incredible!" she said, extending her arms in front of her like a superhero.

Zeke helped her fly around the room, then brought her gently down to the ground.

"I have to say, this is the wildest game of Truth or Dare ever!" said Harris.

After a few more rounds, the game ended. The friends unrolled the sleeping bags and got ready for bed. As Harris headed to the bathroom, he met Zeke coming out. They paused in the hallway.

"I guess tomorrow morning we're going to say goodbye—again. Only this time it really is forever," Harris said sadly.

"I am also sad, Harris," said Zeke. "You turned the worst part of moving to a new planet—trying to make a new friend—into the best part. I will miss you."

Then both boys headed for their sleeping bags.

In the middle of the night, Roxy woke up. She had to go the bathroom, so she slipped out of her sleeping bag. Looking over at Harris, she saw that he was sound asleep. She looked over at Zeke's sleeping bag, but it was empty.

On a hunch, she looked up at the ceiling. There, she saw Zeke, hanging upside down in midair, sound asleep.

I'm glad I got to be friends with a Tragonian, Roxy thought. *I'm sure going to miss him.*

10 GOODBYES AND HELLOS

THE NEXT MORNING, THE three friends sat quietly around the breakfast table.

Harris's mom broke the silence.

"So, your family is going back to Tragas today, Zeke?" she asked.

"Yes," Zeke said sadly.

"Is it a long trip?" she asked.

"Um, yeah, it does take a while," Zeke replied, doing his best not to look at Harris or Roxy.

"Well, we are certainly going to miss you as neighbors," said Harris's mom.

She looked out the window at what had been a bright, sunny morning. Suddenly, the sky darkened and a huge thunderstorm moved in, blocking out the sun.

"It looks like we're having another one of those surprise thunderstorms," she said. "They seem to be happening more often lately."

The three friends looked at each other, knowing that this meant that Zeke's parents had returned from their meeting on Mars.

"I think I should be heading home," said Zeke. "Thank you for everything, Mrs. Walker."

"Harris, why don't you and Roxy walk Zeke home," Harris's mom said. "You can say your goodbyes there."

Walking slowly across the front lawns that connected Harris's house to Zeke's, the three friends remained silent. As they approached Zeke's backyard, the thunderstorm stopped and the skies cleared.

In the backyard, they found Xad and Quar standing in front of the rusty garden shed.

Why did they bother to disguise the spaceship again when we are about to take off for Tragas? Zeke wondered.

"How did your meeting with Supervisor Frow go?" he asked.

Xad and Quar smiled at each other. "We have some news that we think will make you happy, Zeke," said Quar.

"Yes," said Xad. "Supervisor Frow told us that the museum exhibit on Kretlak Prime based on our research of Earth is a huge hit. And so, the Tragonian Science Council wants us to extend our stay here and research other aspects of life on Earth so the museum can expand the exhibit."

Zeke, Harris, and Roxy grabbed each other in a group hug and started jumping up and down.

"That is fantastic news!" said Zeke.

Quar looked right at Harris and Roxy. "And, since you two now know the truth about us and our research, we were hoping that you could help us better study and understand Earth culture."

"Wow!" said Roxy. "You mean, like be your assistants?"

"Yes," said Xad. "Any ideas about new areas for us to research would be most welcome."

"I have an idea," said Zeke. "Have you ever studied the amazing creatures that live underwater in Earth's oceans? There's an animal that lives there that's bigger than a Kraka beast. And another that has more tentacles than we do!"

"We have not," said Quar. "That sounds like a wonderful place to start our next round of research. How did you think of that?"

"Well," said Zeke, looking at Harris and Roxy. "It always helps when you have good friends to inspire you!"

Read on for a sneak peek
from the first book in the
Monster and Me series

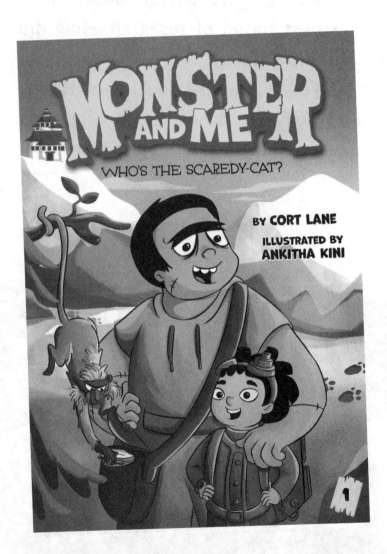

Chapter 1:
Brothers and Best Friends

"**W**AAHOOO!!!" Freddy von Frankenstein zoomed down the mountain in his brand-new, three-wheeled super-cycle! Like most of his favorite things, he had built it himself, and this was his first time taking it for a spin. He couldn't wait to zip over boulders and whoosh straight down the mountain's steep cliffs.

In the passenger seat, Freddy's big brother, F.M., held his stomach. "Can you slow down a bit, Freddy?" F.M. asked, but Freddy was going so fast F.M.'s pleas were lost in the wind.

"This is my best invention yet!" Freddy cried.

"We're gonna have so much fun!"

It wasn't just the super speed of Freddy's super-cycle that scared F.M. He was afraid of A LOT of things: bees, clowns, spiders, thunder, scary movies, fire—you name it!

But he was most afraid of the people who lived in the village at the foot of the mountain. And it seemed that's right where Freddy was headed.

F.M. had never been to the village before. He and Freddy lived in Nepal, high up in the Himalaya Mountains, far away from most people.

Their dad, Victor, had moved to the mountains to keep F.M. safe from humans. Victor von Frankenstein was one of the world's most brilliant scientists, and F.M. was his greatest invention.

Nine years ago, Victor made F.M. in a laboratory in Europe. He used machines and chemicals, and even lightning! And one night,

F.M. was alive! Victor loved F.M., but the townspeople took one look at his huge size and gray skin, and were afraid. Their fear made them unkind. They chased him with torches and called him "Frankenstein's Monster."

F.M. didn't like being called a monster at first. He knew monsters were scary and mean, and he was very, very kind. Over time, he decided that being a "monster" meant that he was unique, and he didn't mind the name so much. But he never forgot how scary and mean the townspeople were to him, and from then on, he was afraid of humans. So Victor found a place where there were no humans around to frighten F.M.

Freddy loved having F.M. as a big brother! Just some reasons why it's so cool:

F.M. gives the best piggyback rides. He can reach stuff in high places. He can throw Freddy in the lake.

He can carry all
of Freddy's inventions
when they conk out.

And he can carry
Freddy when HE conks
out after a long day of
adventures.

He's superstrong and can't
be hurt, even if his huge
hands and feet can make
him a little clumsy.

Who wouldn't want an awesome brother like that?

Journey to some magical places, discover monsters, rock out, and find your inner superhero with these other chapter book series from Little Bee Books!

A. I. NEWTON always wanted to travel into space, visit another planet, and meet an alien. When that didn't work out, he decided to do the next best thing—write stories about aliens! The Alien Next Door series gives him a chance to imagine what it's like to hang out with an alien. And you can do the same—unless you're lucky enough to live next door to a real-life alien!

ALAN BROWN is an artist who whose work includes the Ben 10: Omniverse graphic novels. He has a keen interest in the comic book world; he loves illustrating bold graphic pieces and strips. He works from an attic studio along with his trusty sidekick, Ollie the miniature schnauzer (miniature in size, giant in personality and appetite), and his two sons, Wilf and Teddy.

LOOK FOR MORE BOOKS IN THE *ALIEN NEXT DOOR* SERIES!